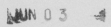

To Elizabeth and Geoffrey Meade

—M.H.

For my mother

—P.B.

Hidden in Sand

Retold by Margaret Hodges

Pictures by Paul Birling

CHARLES SCRIBNER'S SONS · NEW YORK

Maxwell Macmillan Canada · Toronto
Maxwell Macmillan International
New York · Oxford · Singapore · Sydney

In a faraway country, said the teller of tales, there once lived a trader who traveled about, buying and selling. He owned five hundred carts, which he loaded with goods and supplies of wood and water for his drivers and oxen. A pilot led the way, and at his side rode the trader's son, a young boy eager to see the world. The trader rode at the end of the long caravan.

It happened on his travels from east to west that the trader had to cross a great desert of sand. The sand was so fine that it slipped through the fingers of the boy's fist and so deep that the hooves of the oxen sank at every step as they plodded along. The sea of sand swallowed all tracks, and there was no road to follow. The going was hard.

Each day when the sun rose high in the sky, the sand became as hot as the top of a stove. No man or beast could walk on it by day, so the caravan crossed the desert at night. The pilot guided the drivers by watching the North Star and certain other stars to the west.

One night the boy said to the pilot, "I want to learn how you follow the stars. Show me."

But the pilot said, "Be quiet, son of a jackal. Do not bother me."

"At least show me the North Star," said the boy.

The pilot pointed with his whip. "There it is. The North Star must be on our right as we travel west. There are other stars that I watch as well. It is very difficult. Now go back to your father, where you belong. I am tired of your chatter." He pushed the boy out of the cart.

So all night long, night after night, the boy rode with his father at the end of the caravan. Each day at dawn, when the pilot gave the signal to stop, the drivers ranged their carts in a circle and unyoked the oxen. They fed and watered the patient beasts. They built fires to cook rice for themselves. Then they raised tents, and most of the drivers lay down to sleep in the heat of the day. But the boy saw that the pilot sat awake, playing at dice with his friends. After supper when the sand was cool and it was time to travel, the pilot sat yawning, while the drivers put out their campfires and drank once more from their water bags, ready to fold their tents and go on their way.

"Ask the pilot to let me sit with him," the boy begged his father.

But the pilot refused, grumbling, "I cannot do my work with a boy to bother me."

The next day the pilot sat gambling and slept not at all. After supper he
said to the drivers, "Tomorrow we will reach the end of this wilderness
and come to the city. Now we can lighten our loads and travel faster. Pour
out the water and throw away the wood. We will not need them again."

The trader trusted the pilot and let the drivers do as he said. They threw the wood from the carts and poured the water into the sand. When night fell, the pilot raised his arm, pointing west, and the caravan moved forward over the trackless wastes.

Now the pilot was tired out. During the night he fell asleep as he rode. While he slept, the oxen had no one to guide them. Bit by bit, they turned and headed back toward the east from which they had come. All night they kept on their way.

Toward morning the boy, too, slept, riding with his father at the end of the caravan. At dawn he opened his eyes when he heard the pilot shouting, "Stop! Stop!" The call passed from one driver to another all down the line. "Stop! Stop!"

The boy looked at the sky. The stars were fading, but he saw that the North Star was not on their right hand. Now it was on their left.

"We are going the wrong way!" shouted the pilot. "Turn the carts around! Turn the carts around!"

As the drivers turned and formed the carts into line again, the boy
looked around him and saw something strange. It was the shadow of a
wide circle, a circle of sticks and logs covered by drifts of sand. He knew
what it meant.

"This is where we camped yesterday!" the boy said to his father.

The pilot came running. He knelt in the sand and beat his breast in
shame. "My fault! My fault! The sand has swallowed our wood and water.
Alas! Without water we shall die. All is lost!"

The drivers unyoked their carts and raised their tents, but in their
hearts they had no hope. Without water the oxen could not go on.

"Without water all of us will die," said the trader to his son. "But we
must not give up. Wait here until I return."

"My father, let me go too," said the boy. "I may be able to help you."

In the cool of the early morning they set off together, on foot, searching here and there for water among the sloping waves of sand. At last, in a distant valley, the boy's keen eyes saw a clump of desert grass. "Father, there must be water under the grass, is it not true?" he asked. "Otherwise the grass could not live."

"True, my son," said the trader. "Return to the carts and tell the strongest and best men to come. Tell them to bring spades."

The fiery sun was rising higher in the sky, but the boy ran all the way back to the caravan. With dry lips he gave his father's message and led the men to where his father was waiting.

As the trader and his son watched, the men dug down, down under the clump of grass until they came to sand that was packed firm and hard, but still no water appeared. In the deep hole the drivers sweated. Their mouths were parched with thirst. Then the spades struck rock.

"So this is our reward!" cried the men. "All our work for nothing. We shall die here!" They threw down their spades in despair and returned to the caravan.

But the boy climbed down into the hole and knelt, listening. "There is water flowing under the rock," he called to his father. "I will bring a sledgehammer."

Once more the boy returned to the caravan and found the
heavy tool. He began to run toward his father. His eyes were
blinded by the fierce rays of the sun. His feet were burned by the
heat of the sand. When he reached the hole, his father shook his head.
"I cannot wield this hammer," he said. "I am at the end of my strength."

"Let me try," said the boy.

Again he climbed down the steep slope of sand, and as he went, the
sand sifted down with him. He raised the hammer high above his head.
He struck the rock with all his strength. But the rock did not yield. Now it
was almost covered with the sliding sand.

Once again the boy struck a blow.

Suddenly the rock split in two, and a stream of water gushed out. The water rose in the hole so fast that the boy had barely time to climb out before the well was full.

From that well the oxen drank. All the men drank and bathed in the fresh, cool water. They chopped up spare axles and yokes from their carts and built fires to cook their rice.

The boy raised a flag by the well so that other thirsty travelers could find it. The pilot said to him, "Come and sit by me. Tonight I will teach you to follow the stars." And when the sun had set, the boy took his place at the head of the caravan as they went on toward their journey's end.

There the trader and his son told the story. And when they had sold
their goods and returned home, they told it again, so that ever afterward
in all that desert country the boy was remembered as the finder of the well
and the breaker of the rock from which came water in a wilderness of sand.